To market!
To market!

Anushka Ravishankar

Emanuele Scanziani

I'm going to the market
With some money in my pocket
My mother's given me a lot of change

To spend it anywhere for
Anything I care for—
Something funny, nice or even strange

I don't know what to get:
A cheap and tiny pet?
A mouse? A fish? A pigeon? Or a cat?

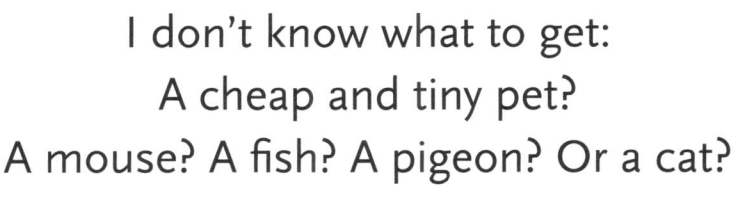

A set of building blocks?
A shiny plastic clock?
A book? A mug? A bucket? Or a hat?

A face-mask, odd and weird?
A false moustache or beard?
A ball? A pot? A basket? Or a bun?

As I think and ponder
I look around and wander
About the market, having lots of fun...

Jangle Jangle Jangle

I'm a bangle-holding stand

Nosy nosy nosy

I'm a posy, I smell grand

I'm a rooster, I can fly

Faster

Faster

Faster

Creeping creeping creeping

I am peeping – I'm a spy

Tutti

tutti

tutti

I'm a fruity kind of dish

Thumping

Thumping

Thumping

I'm a jumping kind of fish

SILLY

SILLY

Silly

SILLY

I'm a chilly sort of sneeze

I am many me's

Funny Funny Funny

Funny Funny Funny

I come back from the market
With the money in my pocket
When my mother asks me: so,
what have you bought?

I give her all the change
And say, Ma, it's very strange
I wonder how it happened;

I FORGOT!

TO MARKET! TO MARKET!

Copyright © 2007 Tara Books
For the text: Anushka Ravishankar
For the illustrations: Emanuele Scanziani
For this edition: Tara Books Pvt. Ltd, India < www.tarabooks.com >
and Tara Publishing Ltd., UK < www.tarabooks.com/uk >

First printing: 2007
Second and Third printing: 2008
This edition 2013

Design: Rathna Ramanathan, Minus9 Design
Production: C. Arumugam
Printed in China through Asia Pacific Offset

ISBN: 978-81-92317-13-7